lo More Singing!

F
Y
C

First published in 2010
by Wayland

Text copyright © Louise John
Illustration copyright © Catalina Alvarez

Wayland
338 Euston Road
London NW1 3BH

Wayland Australia
Level 17/207 Kent Street
Sydney, NSW 2000

Series Editor: Louise John
Editor: Katie Powell
Cover design: Paul Cherrill
Design: D.R.ink
Consultant: Shirley Bickler

A CIP catalogue record for this book is available from the British Library.

ISBN 9780750261883

Printed in China

Wayland is a division of Hachette Children's Books,
an Hachette UK Company

www.hachette.co.uk

No More Singing!

Written by Louise John
Illustrated by Catalina Alvarez

WAYLAND

"Oh, I do like to be beside the seaside!" sang Dad. "I do like to be beside the sea!"

5

"No more singing,"
said Mum. "I feel sick."

"Oh, dear!" said Dad.
"Come and see
the boats."

9

"Oh, I do like to be
beside the seaside!"
sang Dad.

"No more singing," said
Cara. "I feel sick and cold."

"Oh, dear!" said Dad.
"Come and see
the caves."

"I do like to be beside the sea!" sang Dad.

"No more singing," said Olly. "I feel sick and cold and wet."

"Dad, come and see
the fish," said Mum.

"Push!" said Cara
and Olly.

"OK," said Dad.
"No more singing!"

21

Guiding a First Read of
No More Singing!

It is important to talk through the book with the child before they read it alone. This prepares them for the way the story unfolds, and allows them to enjoy the pictures as you both talk naturally, using the language they will later encounter when reading. Read them the brief overview, and then follow the suggestions below:

1. Talking through the book

All the family were on a boat. Dad was enjoying the boat trip and singing loudly. The rest of the family were fed up, but Dad kept on singing. Finally, Olly and Cara found a way to make him stop.

Let's read the title: **No More Singing!**
The family were on a boat on page 4 and Dad was happily singing,
    "Oh, I do like to be beside the seaside!
    I do like to be beside the sea!"
The family don't look happy, though. On page 6, Mum said, "No more singing!" She felt sick.

Continue through the book, guiding the discussion to fit the text as the child looks at the illustrations.

On page 16, Mum decided to play a trick on Dad. She showed him something in the water. Let's turn the page. What happened next? Yes, Cara and Olly pushed Dad in. And on page 20, was he ok? Did he carry on singing?

22

2. A first reading of the book

Ask the child to read the book independently, pointing carefully underneath each word (tracking), while thinking about the story. Praise attempts by the child to correct themselves, and prompt them to use their letter knowledge, the punctuation, and check the meaning, for example:

> **You spotted the word 'be' at the beginning of that word. Does 'beside' make sense? 'Beside' and 'seaside' rhyme, don't they?**

> **Well done. You checked the picture and sounded out 'c-o-l-d' and then you read the sentence again.**

3. Follow-up activities

The high frequency words in this title are:

and   be   come   do   I   like   no   said
see   the   to

- Select two high frequency words, and ask the child to find them throughout the book. Discuss the shape of the letters and their letter sounds.
- To memorise the words, ask the child to write them in the air, then write them repeatedly on a whiteboard or on paper, leaving a space between each attempt.

4. Encourage

- Reading the book again – with expression.
- Drawing a picture based on the story.
- Writing one or two sentences using the practised words.

START READING is a series of highly enjoyable books for beginner readers. **The books have been carefully graded to match the Book Bands widely used in schools.** This enables readers to be sure they choose books that match their own reading ability.

Look out for the Band colour on the book in our Start Reading logo.

The Bands are:

Pink Band 1A & 1B

Red Band 2

Yellow Band 3

Blue Band 4

Green Band 5

Orange Band 6

Turquoise Band 7

Purple Band 8

Gold Band 9

START READING books can be read independently or shared with an adult. They promote the enjoyment of reading through satisfying stories supported by fun illustrations.

Louise John is really the editor of Start Reading, but wanted to see how she liked writing books, too. It was quite tricky, but she found that eating lots of chocolate biscuits made her think better! She tries out her ideas on her daughter, Amelia, who tells her if they are any good or not!

Catalina Alvarez lives in Sherwood, Nottingham with her son Oscar and two cats called Lizzie and Winnie. She has illustrated more books than she can count, especially lots of phonics books. , Her favourite one is called 'Pog the Dog!'

First published 2005
Evans Brothers Limited
2A Portman Mansions
Chiltern St
London W1U 6NR

Text copyright © Vivian French 2005
© in the illustrations Tim Archbold 2005

British Library Cataloguing in Publication Data
French, Vivian
         Pig in love. – (Zig zag)
         1. Children's stories – Pictorial works
         I. Title
         823.9'14 [J]

ISBN 0237529505
13-digit ISBN (from 1 January 2007) 9780237529505

Printed in China by WKT Company Ltd

Series Editor: Nick Turpin
Design: Robert Walster
Production: Jenny Mulvanny
Series Consultant: Gill Matthews

Pig in Love

by Vivian French
illustrated by Tim Archbold

Evans

When Pig fell in love
With Piggie next door
He took her red roses —

Then took her some more.

"I love you, dear Piggie!
I hope you love me!

Why don't we get married?
Please say you agree!"

But Piggie said, "No!"
And started to cry.

"My daddy won't let me
Until pigs can fly!"

Our Pig was a hero.
He made himself wings

Of leather and feathers
And tied them with strings.

He marched to the hill
At the top of the town,

But he couldn't fly up –

17

He could only fly down.

Then Cow floated by
In her spotty balloon,

21

"Hey, you there –
Come with me!
I'm off to the moon!"

23

"Oh YES!" shouted Pig
And his Piggie together,

25

"Let's fly to the moon!

And we'll stay there for ever!"

So Pig and his Piggie
Flew off and away...

Were they happy? You bet!
And they're happy today.

Why not try reading another ZigZag book?

Dinosaur Planet   ISBN: 0 237 52667 0
by David Orme and Fabiano Fiorin

Tall Tilly   ISBN: 0 237 52668 9
by Jillian Powell and Tim Archbold

Batty Betty's Spells   ISBN: 0 237 52669 7
by Hilary Robinson and Belinda Worsley

The Thirsty Moose   ISBN: 0 237 52666 2
by David Orme and Mike Gordon

The Clumsy Cow   ISBN: 0 237 52656 5
by Julia Moffatt and Lisa Williams

Open Wide!   ISBN: 0 237 52657 3
by Julia Moffatt and Anni Axworthy

Too Small   ISBN 0 237 52777 4
by Kay Woodward and Deborah van de Leijgraaf

I Wish I Was An Alien   ISBN 0 237 52776 6
by Vivian French and Lisa Williams

The Disappearing Cheese   ISBN 0 237 52775 8
by Paul Harrison and Ruth Rivers

Terry the Flying Turtle   ISBN 0 237 52774 X
by Anna Wilson and Mike Gordon

Pet To School Day   ISBN 0 237 52773 1
by Hilary Robinson and Tim Archbold

The Cat in the Coat   ISBN 0 237 52772 3
by Vivian French and Alison Bartlett

Pig in Love   ISBN 0 237 52950 5
by Vivian French and Tim Archbold

The Donkey That Was Too Fast   ISBN 0 237 52949 1
by David Orme and Ruth Rivers

The Yellow Balloon   ISBN 0 237 52948 3
by Helen Bird and Simona Dimitri

Hamish Finds Himself   ISBN 0 237 52947 5
by Jillian Powell and Belinda Worsley

Flying South   ISBN 0 237 52946 7
by Alan Durant and Kath Lucas

Croc by the Rock   ISBN 0 237 52945 9
by Hilary Robinson and Mike Gordon